# Dedication

This book is dedicated to everyone who made this book possible.

# Acknowledgments

I could not have done this without the support of my family and friends, the GenKo Sound Co, Genthebuilder, the Shameless Band, Makaila Tonan and Vanessa Montano.

# Boink, boink, boink!
### "Yeah!" The crowd shouts.

"Mommy, what is the crowd shouting about?"
"He won! He won! It is Ruffles, you see. The fastest bunny
rabbit in Fuzzy Furry Forest you will ever meet."

"Ruffles, do tell, how do you run so fast?"
"It is simple, I tell you... I work out three times a day,
eat the best of foods, **never** any trash."
"Three times a day? *Good Sir*, it can't be done."

"Well, you see in the morning, I lift weights with no breaks.

For lunch, I climb trees, and then Sir, *I run, run, run!*"

*Boink, boink, boink!*

Just then, walking from the hills into the forest was the smoothest, coolest bunny rabbit and everyone noticed.

"Ringo Rabbit is the name and winning is my game. I hear you lumps talking about your number one runner, but you don't have this conversation without the *number one gunner*.

I could beat three of you put together. I could beat the best of you with one arm and one leg in the worse of weather."

"What is this nonsense you speak of Ringo Rabbit? I am Ruffles, the most intelligent, fastest rabbit on land, I will beat you then break you like the baddest of bad habits!"

"Is that so, my proper furry friend? I must say you do run quite well, but when it is all over, the fact of the matter is I will win."

"So, shall it be? A race to the finish line? Indeed, a race we must have then victory shall be **mine**."

Then all the animals of Fuzzy Furry Forest came together to chat. Mr. Bear said in his big, deep voice, "I'd beat that Ringo Blingo myself, but I am too fat."

Then the deer said, "You cannot trust an animal that would wear a human backpack."

"No, no, no!" said the wise old owl.

"You all have missed the simple point somehow. This foolish race won't prove a thing... There is no money or property, not even a ring. What we need is a bet to up the ante, a wager of some kind to make the winner feel all his victory. I have just the thing in mind."

"The winner will receive the best of spoils — a royal treatment. Everyone he sees will bow. The loser will take a walk of shame — a loser's lap, so to speak, and then he must leave town."

All at once and at the same exact time, the very thought of losing their beloved Ruffles had entered their minds.

"If Ringo wins, what will we do? What will we do?" Ringo beat Ruffles? I do not think so. Ruffles, he will never lose."

Now all this talk stirred up a great deal of curiosity. No one really knew how fast Ringo could really run, you see.

BJ, the woodpecker and best friend of Ruffles the Rabbit, flew right up to Ringo and said, "Okay, Mr. Ringo I have had it."

"You go around boasting about how fast you run, but me, Bartholomew John Jamerhime, think that you are *done*. Talk is cheap. We have not seen anything, no, not *one*."

"BJ, good fellow, I do not intend to simply talk, but I do assure you, I will indeed walk the walk.

Here, here, everyone please gather around. I will give one of two of the best shows in town."

Proudly, Ringo stood to his feet and said, "Let the show begin. For if you did not know, now you will, I have no choice but to win."

And with no warning at all,
*"poof,"* he was gone.

All the animals gasped as they heard Ringo on the other side of the forest humming and singing his song.

"What will we do? What will we do? Ruffles could never run that fast! He will for surely lose."

Saddened by the thought of his first defeat, "That's it!" Ruffles said. "Those things on his feet. We must, we must acquire a pair! I will beat him at his own game with no feelings to spare."

"Oh Ruffles, this is your grandest idea of all. And I, Bartholomew John Jamerhime will be there to see the fall. That pompous Ringo has no clue and has no mind of what we plan to do."

"I will wear those springs, bouncing about, then I will sing! Victory, oh, sweet victory. But we need them now. I need those springs. I will get them somehow. But how would I get them without breaking the law?

Would it really matter if I took them and no one saw? I could just borrow them and make a pair of my own. I will take them in the dark and no one will know."

Late that night when all were asleep, Ruffles made his way to Ringo without making a peep. The springs that would win him the race were now in his hands.

*Just as he was leaving, he began to understand.*

The thought of victory, the joy to win. But was it worth committing the Rabbit's ultimate sin of sins? At that very moment, Ruffles had begun to see — if he were to win the race that it would not truly be a victory.

*"What I have to do is win fair and square, and if I lose, he will be the better hare."*

The very next day when the race began, the crowd was full with no room in the stands. Ruffles lost the race that day with fashion and style, but he won something even greater that would last him all the while.

Ruffles learned to be a good sport, win or lose.
And when it comes to cheating, there is no question what Ruffles will choose.

THE END

81353419R00017